Flight of the Blue Serpent

A Magical World Awaits You

Read

THE
SECRETS
—OF—
DROON

THE SECRETS OF DROON

— TONY ABBOTT —

Flight of the Blue Serpent

Illustrated by Royce Fitzgerald
Cover illustration by Tim Jessell

SCHOLASTIC INC.
New York Toronto London Auckland Sydney
Mexico City New Delhi Hong Kong Buenos Aires

To those whose
imaginations take flight
with every book they read

For more information about the continuing saga of Droon,
please visit Tony Abbott's Web site at
www.tonyabbottbooks.com.

ISBN-13: 978-0-439-90254-0
ISBN-10: 0-439-90254-1

12 11 10 9 8 7 6 5 4 3 2 1   8 9 10 11 12 13/0

Printed in the U.S.A.
First printing, October 2008

Contents

One

Storm in the North

"Hold on tight, everyone. We're going in!" cried Keeah as her four-winged, dome-topped flying ship, the *Dragonfly*, plunged into the thickening snows of Droon's far north.

Sitting snug inside the ship next to Keeah were Eric Hinkle and his friends Neal and Julie. Behind them sat Keeah's mother, Queen Relna, and the blue-faced

Orkins, Djambo and his gray-haired elder, Mudji.

The friendly spider troll, Max, was in front next to Galen Longbeard, Droon's oldest and most powerful wizard. And hunched in the very nose of the ship was the frizzy-haired and bespectacled pilot, Friddle.

Making the ship all the more cozy was the fact that each passenger was dressed from boots to cap to mittens in the thickest winter furs.

The snowy north of Droon was unlike anywhere in his world, Eric reflected as he gazed out the *Dragonfly*'s round portals. Droon was the land of adventure and magic that he, Julie, and Neal had discovered one day under his basement. They loved Droon. The three had even developed wizard powers like those of their Droon friends Galen, Relna, and Keeah.

But they had never traveled so far north before.

"And there to your left," said Friddle, busily working the controls, "is the treacherous Paraneshi Iceway, home of the legendary Nesh ice warriors. We're far past Silversnow now, my friends. Below us lies a forbidding and uncharted wasteland."

"A wasteland indeed," said Galen. "But one that holds mysteries and secrets."

"And treasures!" said Mudji.

Each of the Dragonfly's passengers knew exactly what the old Orkin meant. The treasure pouch on Eric's belt was the reason they were flying into the stormy north.

According to Mudji, a hundred years before, a storm just like the one they were now entering had split the sky in two, creating a rare passage between the worlds.

A strange blue serpent entered Droon

through the passage. It crashed in the storm, and one of the serpent's snowflake-shaped scales fell to earth. Sensing that the blue snowflake contained magical power, young Mudji hid it away from those who might use it for evil. The snowflake became known as the "Orkin Treasure."

For years the treasure lay buried. And so it would have remained, but Ko, the fierce ruler of the beasts, found it.

Only through Galen's cleverness was Ko foiled and the treasure now in their hands. But the wizard feared that the passage would open again, and he was convinced that the snowflake and the legend of the serpent were but two elements of a larger story. So now Galen was leading this expedition into the north to discover the truth.

"Can we go any faster?" asked Relna, looking out the window ports to the ground below. "The storm will soon be at its peak and we must be there to protect the passage."

Friddle nodded. "Strap yourselves in, my friends. Faster means rougher!"

As the ship rattled and shook, Eric opened the pouch and drew out the strange blue snowflake. Keeah, Julie, and Neal looked on as the glow of the plane's wall lamps played over the treasure's shiny surface.

If the flake were made of snow, Eric imagined that it was some sort of magic snow, for it didn't melt. The treasure was the size of a medallion, bore twelve crystalline points, and was very thin. But when he held it, it felt heavy, and it seemed to breathe with a power he could only guess at.

"It's beautiful," said Max. "What magic do you think it has? What does it do?"

Keeah shook her head. "I wonder if we'll ever know. It may always be a mystery."

"I think it has powers," said Neal, his turban perched on his head like a dollop of whipped cream. "Don't ask me what kind."

"What I don't get is how a serpent entered Droon from *our* world," said Julie. "We don't have serpents. We never had serpents!"

"Unless you count Mr. Higgens," said Neal. "He hisses whenever I cut across his yard."

To Eric, the flake was more than magical and otherworldly. It enticed him and frightened him at the same time, just as its power simultaneously warmed and chilled his skin.

"Maybe the serpent needs it in order to fly," he said. "Maybe it's been waiting a hundred years for the passage to open again, and it needs this scale to fly home."

Galen's forehead wrinkled in thought. "Very possible, Eric. No doubt we shall discover this and more secrets very soon."

Too soon, thought Eric.

For there was something else about the treasure. It was more than simply a mysterious object. The snowflake held a terrifying prophecy.

Thinking back, Eric recalled the frightening words of Emperor Ko.

"This tiny treasure will do no less than unite all the sons of Zara in a single place and time. A place and time when they are most vulnerable. And one of them . . . one of them . . . will fall. . . ."

The sons of Zara! thought Eric. As he watched Galen, whose eyes were fixed on the treasure, he knew the wizard feared the danger to himself and his brothers,

Sparr and Urik, if the prophecy were to come true.

Of course, the friends had discussed the prophecy over and over on the long way north and had decided that it really was impossible. It was inconceivable that all the sons of Zara could gather in the same place and time.

Due to the odd magic of time travel, Lord Sparr was now very old and blind, and had been missing for months and months.

And Urik was trapped in time, not in Droon at all, but in the Upper World. The last thing anyone knew, Urik was lost between 1572 and 1904, when Sparr fought him for the magical Moon Medallion.

The prophecy didn't add up.

And Eric was glad it didn't.

And yet . . . and yet . . . he couldn't get it out of his mind. As he held the snowflake in his palm, he felt that this journey to the north was no less than a race against time, in which all the elements — the snowflake, the storm, the serpent, and the prophecy — would combine in a way no one could imagine.

"There it is!" Mudji said, pointing to a snowcapped ring of mountains below the ship. "That valley is where the serpent fell!"

"Circle and land, Friddle, if you please," said Galen.

"Aye-aye!" said the pilot, and the *Dragonfly* plowed downward through the battering winds.

"Mudji," said Keeah, still gazing at the blue snowflake, "before we land, please tell us again what you know about this treasure."

"Ah, yes!" Closing his eyes, the elder Orkin began to recollect his past of a century before. "As you know, Orkins were once Ninns," he said. "And I was still a young Ninn warrior on patrol in the far north when a wild storm suddenly flared up. The sky cracked open and a great blue serpent flew into our world!"

"You must have been scared," said Max.

"Terrified!" said Mudji. "All at once lightning flashed — baboom! — and the serpent fell. I tried to run but was struck on the shoulder by this very snowflake, which I believe is no less than one of the serpent's scales!"

"Did it hurt?" asked Neal.

"Hurt, nothing!" said the Orkin. "No sooner did it strike me than — poof! — I lost my Ninn shape and became . . . an Orkin!"

The *Dragonfly* dipped suddenly. Wind rattled its windows. Gusts of blinding snow slammed it from every direction.

Leaning forward, Friddle gripped the wheel tightly. "My friends, we must land now, or be forced to land. And by that I mean crash!"

"*Crash* is not my favorite word," said Neal. "I say land."

"We *all* say land," said Relna. She pointed to a stretch of flat ground leading to the crest of the valley. "Can you put us there?"

"I'll try," said Friddle. At once, he banked the *Dragonfly* and brought it in swiftly.

Just before they touched down, however, something flashed through the air and struck the plane's windshield — *blam!*

The object shattered upon impact.

"This storm is crazy!" Eric gasped.

A second object struck the airship.

Then another and another. *Blam! Blam!*

"This is not the storm," said Galen, scanning the hills below. "Those shots came from . . . down there!"

Another powerful shot blasted the ship, and the engine began to sputter.

"It's . . . it's . . . an icicle!" cried Friddle. "We're being attacked with icicles!"

"Icicles?" said Neal. "You mean the kind that break off rooftops?"

Cling! Plink! Clonk!

"No, I mean the kind that crash planes!" said Friddle.

"Our enemies are already here!" said Relna, holding tightly to her seat.

Another volley of ice daggers struck the plane, and the engine flamed out.

"Friddle was right about a rough landing!" said Max. "Hold tight to whatever you can find!"

And the *Dragonfly*, crippled and powerless, fell to earth amid a hail of ice daggers.

Two

Ice Bones

If the frizzy-haired inventor had not been such a good pilot, the *Dragonfly*'s crew might not have survived its emergency landing.

As it was, Friddle was able to bounce the plane to a stop near the rim of the ice valley.

"Let's defend ourselves!" cried Galen.

They all jumped out of the plane and

took shelter behind it, scanning for attackers amid the whirling snow.

"The icicles came from behind those snowdrifts," said Keeah, her fingertips sparking as she pointed to several wind-blown hedges that ringed the valley.

Blam! Clonk! Icicles shattered on the plane's nose, then on its tail, and then on the ground behind the children.

"We're surrounded," said Julie.

"On every side!" said Neal.

"That's what surrounded means!" Julie cried.

"I just wanted to be clear," said Neal.

"You'll be clear, all right," said Eric. "As clear as a ghost, unless we get out of here! I see a pass leading down into the valley."

"Follow me!" yelled Galen. He thrust his staff into the snowstorm and jerked it once.

Whoooom! A tunnel pierced its way through the wild wind and snow.

"Hurry to safety," urged Max.

The friends hastened into Galen's magic tunnel, heading toward a narrow pass in the hills surrounding the valley.

But they didn't get far.

The sound of scraping and rattling filled the frigid air as strange creatures rushed one by one out of the madly driving snow.

"What are those things?" asked Neal.

Those things were odd, tall beings wobbling on frames no thicker than the width of a bone. They looked like skeletons with broad shoulders that were hung with icicles. They were all bones and joints, with heads no wider than their limbs.

But that wasn't their strangest part. The creatures were made entirely of icicles!

"Icemen?" said Max.

"The worst kind!" said Mudji. "These are the legendary Nesh warriors! They are not often seen this far north. They are the oddest creatures, and that's why. Look!"

The friends watched, dumbstruck, as the ice warriors reached up to their bony shoulders and snapped off spears of hanging ice. Taking aim, they hurled the icicles directly at the friends.

Clink! Clank! Galen whacked the icicles with his staff. They exploded, showering the children with a spray of ice crystals.

"Ayeee-iiii!" the creatures shrieked.

"Djambo, Mudji, Friddle, to the ground. Wizards, in position!" shouted Keeah. She shot blast after blast at the icicle men.

Relna and Galen stood side by side with her and followed suit. Julie and Neal huddled together behind Eric as he sprayed silver sparks at the warriors. But with each blast, Eric was aware of something he had feared ever since his magic had returned.

While the flashes of silver light that shot from his fingertips were bright and strong, his abilities simply weren't as powerful as before.

It took more of him to do less.

He still saw visions, of course. In one vision he had even seen the blue snowflake before it was found. But he felt he wasn't the young wizard he once was. Something had changed.

Maybe *he* had changed.

"Help!" Max yelled. He dived to avoid an ice dagger and tumbled into Eric, pushing them both helplessly across the ice. A troop of icy skeleton men bore down on them.

"Eric, blast them!" cried Max. Eric aimed his fingers. A stream of silver sparks shot out, then dissolved in the air.

"What?" cried Max. "Eric —"

"Nesh fiends, be gone!" shouted Galen, whirling his staff at the charging warriors.

Fwank! Fooom! Bits of ice sprayed out like frozen rain, while larger shards flew against the sides of the hills behind them and crackled into dust.

The ice warriors, moaning and squealing, retreated into the storm and were gone.

The valley ledge was quiet.

Eric wanted to say something, but Max spoke first. "Thank you, Galen! Eric and I were trapped, and you saved us!"

Galen patted the spider troll's shoulder. "A wizard's duty is to protect those he loves." He turned to Eric. "Your powers . . ."

"I'm having trouble," said Eric. "When Salamandra's spell took them from me, and I got them back, it was . . . I don't know . . ."

"Too easy?" said Galen.

Eric nodded. "I think so. I feel I can't defend myself. Or anyone else."

"Wizards grow neither easily nor quickly," said Galen. "Often a loss of magic becomes a test for a wizard. Perhaps your test —"

The wizard stopped abruptly, turned, and appeared to be listening to something.

Eric listened, too. He heard the wind sweeping wildly across the wasteland. But was there something else, another sound?

Tapping? Was there . . . a tapping noise?

Galen breathed deeply. Saying nothing, he simply nodded to himself, then grasped his staff tightly and walked on.

"The storm worsens," said Mudji. "Let us enter the valley where the serpent fell."

"And speaking of falling," said Friddle, looking back at the damaged plane, "our landing was quite rough. The *Dragonfly* is in need of some work. . . ."

"Quite right," said Relna. "Friddle, you and I shall repair the ship. Something tells me we'll need it sooner rather than later. Galen, will you lead the others?"

The wizard bowed. "Of course. We have an hour or two before the storm reaches its peak. Eric, do you have the snowflake?"

Eric patted the leather pouch at his side. "Safe and sound."

"Do not let it out of your sight," said Galen. "Now let's be off."

Mudji acted as guide, walking side by side with Djambo, Keeah, Neal, and Julie. Galen strode by himself, and Eric and Max brought up the rear. Winds swirled over them as they climbed into the pass that led down to the valley.

After a time, Eric felt a tap on his arm. He turned. Max was looking at him.

"I saw Galen the other day," the spider troll whispered. "He was consulting maps, timetables, histories of Droon, moon charts. All of a sudden, he went into a trance."

"What do you imagine he was thinking about?" asked Eric.

Max shook his head. "I don't know. But it's clear something is worrying him."

Eric wondered if the wizard knew something they didn't. Could the dark prophecy come true after all? Was that what they were all moving toward? A gathering of the sons of Zara? But how was it possible? No one knew where Sparr and Urik were. How could the treasure draw them all to the same place, anyway? What kind of magic did it have?

"I don't know," said Eric.

"At least he is there to help us when we need it, no?" Max said. "You heard him. A wizard's duty is to protect those he loves."

Eric wanted to thank Galen for helping him, but the wizard seemed to want to be alone. So Eric hung back.

Before long the little band entered a circle of hills so tall that their tops were barely visible through the snowfall.

"It's here I saw the serpent go down," said Mudji. "The legend begins here!"

The valley around them looked at first like a random cluster of frost heaves and ice mounds, ledges and shelves and outcroppings of snow, with caves burrowed out of solid white hills by ferocious winds and storms. But the more the friends looked, the more they realized it was not random at all.

Between one ice mound and a cave was a tamped-down road. Coiling up one giant frost heave was a crude set of stairs.

The farther they descended into the valley, the more the friends saw. Domed dwellings with holes like windows were stacked up the sides of snow peaks. In the drifts between them were the marks of tiny feet and innumerable wheel tracks.

Galen halted. "I hear noises."

Eric wondered if Galen heard the same sounds as before. Then he heard them, too.

Spsss . . . sss?

Mudji laughed. "Can it be my old friends? The snowfolk? After all these years? Come out. Show yourselves!"

Then, from behind ice boulders, drifts, and mounds, came dozens of creatures as round as they were tall.

"Snowfolk!" said Djambo. "The noblest people of the north!"

The snowfolk were plump, round-faced men, women, and children. The men had snowy white beards down to the tops of their snowy white boots.

One of them stepped forward and bowed. "Welcome to Krone," he said. "I am Baggle. Krone is here. For us. For you."

"Thank you," said Galen. "We have traveled from the far south. We have just been attacked by ice warriors."

Baggle nodded grimly. "You saw Nesh. Yucky icemen. We call them Yugs."

"Yugs?" said Neal. "I like the name."

"They attack. To find," said the man.

"To find?" asked Keeah. "To find what?"

"Serpent," said Baggle.

"The serpent!" said Mudji, his eyes wide with wonder. "I told you!"

"We have come because of the legend," said Max. "Have you seen the serpent? Is it quite blue?"

"Never seen," said Baggle, wrinkling his brow.

"No, no, never," said another little snowperson.

"Legend tells of blue color," said Baggle.

"Quite blue," said the other.

"And we hear it," said Baggle.

"Yes, yes, always," said the other. "Calling from below. From icy room. Enchanted room. Filled with music. Music!"

The friends looked at one another.

"Are you saying that you hear the serpent? Is it living below your city?" asked Keeah.

"And serpent master, too," said Baggle. "Speaks words. Have never seen."

"A voice?" said Galen. "What does it say?"

" 'Help blue serpent. Find what is lost,' "
said Baggle.

"Lost?" said Eric. "Could he mean the treasure? Baggle, we brought a treasure with us. It was lost for many years. We think it came from the serpent."

Baggle's eyes grew wide when he saw the snowflake. "Blue. Like serpent —"

All of a sudden, a giant snowball hurtled down the street directly at the children.

"Out of the way!" shouted Neal. He dived to the side of the path, pushing Eric into a drift, completely burying him.

"Dude," said Neal. "That could have hurt."

"It did," said Eric, brushing snow from his coat collar and sleeves.

The giant snowball stopped and unwrapped itself. It was another of the little people, with a shorter beard than Baggle's.

"Reporting!" he said with a salute.

"What is?" asked Baggle.

"Snowfolk in trouble!" said the man.

"Not caravan?" asked Baggle.

"Yes caravan!" said the other. "Trapped on frozen lake. Yugs will find. Yugs will hurt!"

Baggle stroked his beard, then nodded. "Friends need help. We go. We help. Now!"

"We'll help, too," said Julie.

"You bet," said Neal. "I'd love a chance to stop those bony icicle throwers."

"Good," said Baggle. "We plan now."

While the friends and the snowfolk huddled together, trying to find a way to help the trapped caravan, Max nudged Eric.

"Look at our friend," he said, pointing to Galen. The wizard was moving slowly away from them and into one of the ice caves, as if drawn toward a sound the others could not hear.

"Let's see where he goes," said Max.

Eric and Max entered the cave. They turned one corner, two corners, until they found the wizard mumbling softly to himself. "Left five steps . . . turn . . ."

"Uh . . . Galen?" said Eric.

"The wall, you say?" Galen whispered. He turned to a solid wall and put his ear to it.

"Is everything quite all right?" said Max.

Galen did not respond, but instead placed one hand firmly against the wall.

"Knock, knock. You guys in there?" Neal called from outside the cave. He, Keeah, and Julie approached the others.

"We've decided how to free the trapped snowfolk," said Keeah. "With some magic."

"What is Galen doing?" asked Julie.

Galen was now moving his hand back and forth across the wall, as if clearing a window of fog.

"It looks like he's waving at someone," whispered Neal. "But it's only a blank wall."

Just then, the wizard set his staff down, placed his other hand next to the first, and pushed at the wall with all his might.

"Oh! Light!" Galen gasped. He looked at Eric. Then, right before their eyes, he fell forward.

He fell *forward* — against the wall, into the wall, and through the wall. And then, he was gone!

"Galen!" cried Eric, pushing on the rock, but finding it completely solid. "Galen!"

As if in response to its owner's name, the staff flared, then flickered and went out.

"He vanished," said Julie. "He's — gone!"

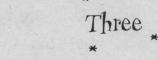

Three

Hoodwinked!

"Galen?" squealed Max, pushing on the cave wall from top to bottom. "Galen!"

"Where did he go?" asked Keeah.

Eric ran his fingers over the rock, but found nothing to tell him where Galen had gone. "There's no opening at all. How did he do it?"

"No time." A voice sniffled.

Baggle waddled into the passage breathlessly, followed by the two Orkins. "Must hurry," Baggle said. "Help friends now. Need them back here. Krone cannot defend itself."

Djambo and Mudji exchanged looks.

"I can help secure Krone while you rescue them," said Djambo. "There is enough Ninn in me to know how to defend a city."

Mudji nodded. "In me, too! Being a red warrior was long ago, but I forget nothing!"

The two blue-faced Orkins slapped their hands together and hustled outside to prepare for the city's defense.

"Come now," Baggle said. "Snowfolk help snowfolk. Must hurry to caravan!"

"Eric, take Galen's staff," said Max. "We may not know where he has gone, but our duty is clear. We must help the snowfolk and find Galen later."

"Right." Eric took the curved staff, and — as every time before — he felt the wizard's magic flow through it. He was grateful for its strength now more than ever.

Together the little band hurried down ice paths and snowpacked trails until they found themselves at a low row of stables. Baggle opened the gates of each stall.

Instead of groggles or pilkas or any other kind of animal, the children saw . . . sleds.

Every sled had silver wings rising off the back. And on the front, there were long pipes arching out of an odd arrangement of pots and cones and tubes.

"Where are the pilkas?" asked Julie.

Baggle grinned. "Pilkas don't like north. Not *many* like north!"

With a touch of his hand, Baggle started one of the devices. A terrible coughing noise was followed by a low, steady hum.

"Sleds," he said. "To find friends."

"*Power* sleds to find friends!" said Neal.

The children climbed on board four sleek iron sleds. Max jumped up with Neal.

"How do we steer them?" asked Keeah.

Baggle chuckled. "Lean!" he said. "Lean there. Sled goes there! Follow me."

He mounted his own sled and leaned forward. The rails slid across the snow.

"Awesome!" said Neal. "Sleds, ho!"

The children followed Baggle. Picking up speed the farther forward they leaned, the small band raced over the ground. Wings of ice sprayed high behind them.

"Did you build the sleds?" asked Max.

Baggle shook his head. "Awoke one day. Sleds were in stables. Gifts for us."

Eric turned to him. "From whom?"

"I will tell," said Baggle. "Big storm came. Big storm went. Then sounds started."

"Sounds?" said Keeah. "From the serpent?"

"Serpent injured," said Baggle. "Hurt in the storm." He raised his hand, and the crew gradually slowed to a stop. His keen eyes gazed into the snowy distance. To the children, the landscape was all the same, white against white, with barely a line or a shape to tell near from far.

But Baggle nodded, satisfied, and pointed to the left. "Caravan. In canyon. There."

He set off, making a wide arc to the left, and was soon speeding across the icy wastes faster than before.

"Then one night — boom! — tall tower appeared!" he said, continuing his story. "Straight from snow! Then more. Boom-boom! Krone was born. Home for us!"

"You mean Krone was built by some-one you never saw?" asked Keeah. "Was it the serpent master? Did he build the city for you?"

Baggle nodded. "Voice came. 'Here is home. Protect my serpent! Find what is lost.' We said, 'Okay.' Have searched. Have not found what is lost."

Eric wondered if Galen had heard this same voice. Had it led him to the enchanted room? Had the serpent master *called* Galen to him?

"What does he sound like?" Eric asked.

"Like music," said Baggle. "Sad music from below. Hush. We are near."

The team of sleds soon came over a high ridge of ice and entered a break in the hills that marked the opening of an ice canyon. In the center they saw the caravan stranded on an island of ice surrounded by dark moving water.

"Trapped on ice," said Baggle. "We go!"

The friends raced their sleds through the pass and onto the floor of the canyon toward the lakeshore. Then, suddenly, Neal slowed down.

"Wait," he said, turning his turbaned head this way and that. "My genie sense tells me something isn't right. I don't like it."

Baggle frowned. "Nor me."

Eric felt something, too. With one hand on the treasure pouch and the other on Galen's staff, he looked around in every direction.

At first, he saw nothing but snow. Then, out of the corner of his eye, he spied a glimmer of light above the canyon entrance behind him.

"Guys . . . the Yugs . . ." he said.

All at once, a thunderous avalanche barreled down the canyon walls, sealing the entrance the children had just come through.

"We've been tricked!" cried Keeah. "The Yugs lured us into the canyon."

"Then shut the door on us," said Neal.

"Yugs trap us!" gasped Baggle, scowling at the sealed pass. "To attack Krone!"

"And not only Krone," said Max. "The Yugs are attacking us, too!"

A terrible shriek — *"Ayeee-iiii!"* — echoed from the far side of the canyon. It sounded like the squeal of ice shattering. The next moment, a great troop of skeleton warriors sped across the snowy wastes on icicle skis. Half were heading toward the trapped snowfolk, and the other half toward the kids.

"They sure are ugly," said Neal.

"And they sure are coming!" cried Keeah.

The Great Ice Conflict

"We need to help the snowfolk," said Eric.

"I know a spell," said Keeah.

While the Yugs came ever closer, Keeah uttered a charm, and the moving water hardened from the shore to the stranded snowfolk. Together, the children, Max, and Baggle drove their sleds across the frozen water and joined the caravan.

Baggle hugged his friends. "Together now. But not safe. Must battle Yugs!"

"My turn," said Neal. Pulling his turban low, he twirled on one heel while mumbling a genie charm. A ring of snow ten feet high descended around the Yugs, trapping them inside. The creatures shrieked in rage.

"And we get out the way we came," said Julie.

"I'll blast the pass clear with Galen's staff," said Eric.

But before they could move, they saw dozens of gangly ice warriors climbing on one another's backs behind the snow wall. More and more joined them until together they formed a single giant pyramid of Yugs.

"Are they going to cheer?" asked Neal.

"Somehow I doubt it," said Julie.

As the children watched, the Yugs

melted into one another, creating one enormous iceman. It towered above them and stepped easily over Neal's snow wall.

"I never saw that coming," said Neal.

"Big Yug!" said Baggle.

The giant Yug stood there, scanning the children and the snowfolk. Then all at once it pointed at Eric and shrieked. "*Ayieee-iiii!*"

Eric gulped. "Me? Why me? I —"

Then he knew. He had the treasure!

"That's what this is about," he gasped. "They want the treasure!"

"Snowfolk, onto the sleds. Let's go!" Keeah said. "We need to get out of here — fast!"

The little people scrambled onto the sleds as quickly as they could.

Eric glanced around and realized that the only way to escape was to slide between the giant's huge feet.

"To the pass!" he said. "Follow me!"

Together the sleds raced right toward the giant. At first the great Yug seemed confused, then it simply crouched and jumped up into the air.

"Is it doing exercises?" said Neal. "I guess even giant Yugs have to keep in shape —"

Then the giant landed.

Crackkkkkk!

When it struck the ground, the big Yug shattered into many parts, and the troop of Yug warriors was back.

"Yugs everywhere!" cried Baggle.

"We're completely surrounded," said Neal.

"On every side!" said Julie.

"That's what I'm talking about!" said Neal.

The Yugs hurled ice daggers through the air — *fwit! fwit! fwit!* — but no sooner had they cracked off bits of themselves than — *slurch!* — the icicles grew back and the warriors were whole again.

Driving first one way then another, the kids' sleds retreated from the ice warriors. But they were soon backed against the canyon wall with nowhere to go.

"There are too many of them," said Julie.

Keeah shot a spray of sparks that acted like a shield. The warriors' daggers shattered against it as long as she held it up.

"Yugs attack us. Yugs attack Krone. Cannot let serpent master down," said Baggle, his jaw set tight. "Children take treasure. Return to Krone. Bring to serpent. We will fight."

It was amazing to Eric that Baggle's first thoughts were for the well-being of the serpent and its master. He admired how the little people — even while fending off an attack — always thought of others first.

"You can't stay here alone," said Eric.

"They won't," said Max. "I'll help them."

"And I will, too," said Keeah, still spraying her shield of sparks. "Eric and Neal, you escape with the treasure. Take it to Krone. We'll hold them off."

"We can do it," Julie agreed.

"But —" Eric started.

"No buts," said Max. "If Galen isn't here, we must imagine what he would do. I think he would say that victory lies in cleverness. We'll create a cover while you sneak away."

Eric looked at Neal. "Well," he said, "the genie hat makes you sort of clever."

Neal grinned. "And you've always been pretty good at sneaking. Let's do it!"

The Yugs kept up their attack on Keeah's wall. With a word, she paused her spell, and the shield vanished.

"Ready — go!" she yelled.

Even as the Yugs tumbled toward them, Eric and Neal hopped onto one sled and drove it straight past the creatures and up over a snowdrift.

"Now we zigzag!" Neal yelped. He leaned from side to side, while Eric, using Galen's staff like an engine, shot a powerful spray behind the sled. It skittered over the ground toward the snow-filled pass.

Whoosh-whoosh-whoosh! The sledders confused the Yugs. At least at first.

Before they knew it, a half-dozen ice warriors, pointing at Eric and his treasure pouch, were diving across the ice like rockets. With a swiftness Eric could not believe, the Yugs charged the sled, pelting Neal with chunks of ice — and forcing him to change course swiftly.

Too swiftly. The sled spun up over a drift and tumbled onto its side. The force of the collision tore the treasure pouch from Eric's belt. It flew across the ground.

"No!" he yelled.

With blurring speed, all six Yugs dived across the snow. They scooped the pouch out of the drift. They raised their arms in victory and howled — *Ahhh-yeeee-ahhh!* — then slid speedily away across the snow.

"After them!" said Eric. He scrambled to the sled and pushed it upright, then Neal leaped on and leaned far forward.

When Eric blasted the snow with Galen's staff, the silver-winged sled took off after the Yugs as fast as it could go.

Five

Strange Treasure

Flying over the snow, the two friends soon found themselves on a narrow trail between steep snow hills.

They spotted the Yug thieves. Eric extinguished Galen's staff and joined Neal at the sled's handles.

"Careful, the ground is way slippery," said Neal as they gained on the six treasure thieves.

"But don't slow down," said Eric. He wasn't sure why, but he wasn't thinking of his own safety as much as his promise to Galen. To keep the treasure safe, he had to get it back. Nothing would stop him.

As they raced along, Eric became aware of a strange, repeating sound.

Tap . . . slish . . . tap . . . slish . . .

"Do you hear that?" he asked Neal.

Neal listened for a moment. "No. But I see that rock. Watch out —"

Suddenly, their sled struck a rock and flew off the path. It slammed into the ice and began to spin around and around like a top. It took both boys' strength not to be thrown off. The sled finally stopped in a snowdrift.

"I guess it was a little icy," Eric said.

"You think?" said Neal. Then he grew quiet. "Holy cow. Take a look!"

Eric saw something glimmer slowly among the nearby rocks. The Yugs were no longer running. They had stopped.

Eric tapped Neal's arm. "Come. Sneak."

"You sound like Baggle," Neal whispered.

Eric smiled. He *did* sound like Baggle, and that was just fine with him. Baggle was as noble as anyone he'd ever met.

The two friends crept through the drifts until they heard the ice warriors mumbling and hissing among themselves. The treasure pouch was sitting on the ground before them.

Then, amid the ice warriors' babble, one word was spoken that they both understood.

"*Pess-pah-met-nee-ala-Ko* —"

"Whoa, dude," whispered Neal. "Ko!"

Ko, thought Eric. Ko, whose prophecy about the snowflake had never left his mind.

One of the Yugs grunted when Ko's name was mentioned. The others growled fearfully, then stepped back from the pouch. They closed it without looking in.

Neal turned to Eric. "Did you see that? They're afraid of Ko. They must be working for him"

Eric nodded. "As usual, Ko has bad guys all over Droon. These guys don't want to anger him by opening the pouch before he does."

"Which may mean he's coming for it," said Neal. "Maybe he's coming for it soon."

The thought made Eric shiver. Did Emperor Ko really think the treasure would magically unite the sons of Zara? Had he known that the blue snowflake would bring Galen up north? Did he suspect that Sparr would turn up there, too?

And what of Urik, the eldest of Zara's sons? He was trapped in the past of the

Upper World. How could he possibly appear after so long? It wasn't even certain he was alive.

Was the prophecy nonsense?

Or was it Ko's most evil trap ever?

"We need it back," said Neal.

"But how?" asked Eric. "There are six of them, plus who knows how many others nearby. We have to look before we leap."

Neal turned to him. "Or the other way around. I may be a genie, but I'm still me. What would Neal do in a situation like this?"

Eric thought for a moment, then smiled. "Create an outrageous distraction?"

"While you grab the treasure!" said Neal.

Eric grinned. "So how Nealish are you feeling today?"

"Very," Neal said. Then, taking handfuls

of snow, he bolted up out of hiding and shouted, "Who wants a snowball fight?"

The ice warriors turned in shock.

"No one?" said Neal. "Then I'll start!" And he hurled snowballs like a machine gun.

At the same time, Eric leaped from his hiding place, dived at the treasure, and snatched it from them.

Shrieking, the thieves jumped at Eric.

But Neal was ready for them. "Wait. Have more genie treats!" Conjuring fireballs from his fingers, he tossed them at the ice creatures. They shrieked and fled into the snow.

"Eric, run!" he said. "I'll chase them!"

Neal whooped loudly, flinging fireballs at the Yugs' feet over and over, chasing them from drift to drift until they disappeared into the storm.

"Thanks, Nealie," whispered Eric.

Then he looked down. The treasure pouch sat unopened in his hands.

He realized he was trembling. Could the strange snowflake actually unite the wizards? Could it find Sparr? Could it find Urik, the most mysterious of Zara's sons?

Eric had a fleeting memory of Urik's smile as the two had soared across rooftops to escape a band of creepy goblins. Urik said he simply imagined himself a bird, and he flew.

As it turned out, Urik had flown right out of their lives — into a whirling time tunnel, not to be seen again.

If the prophecy *could* come true, Eric had to make sure it was safe. Slowly, he pulled the pouch open, knowing he was doing what the icemen had refused to do.

He put his hand into the pouch, closed his fingers over the treasure, and pulled it out.

He gasped. "What?"

It was not the blue snowflake.

What lay in his palm was the size and weight of the snowflake, but was no more than a plain round disc, flat, shiny, and colored a bluish white. In its center was a small blue knob or button. And instead of twelve crystalline points, it bore twelve black marks around its edge. It looked like a dial or the face of a cheap clock.

Eric fell to his knees. "No, no, no!" he gasped. "Where is the snowflake? How could the Yugs have switched it? What *is* this thing? What about the prophecy?"

Then the noise came again.

Tap . . . slish . . . tap . . . slish . . .

Listening, Eric wrapped the pouch on

his belt again. Then, bracing himself with Galen's staff, he rose to his feet.

The air was quiet. He listened.

Tap . . . slish . . .

Eric turned. "What *is* that?"

The sound faded away. Then another sound came. It was close by.

Erch . . . erch . . . erch!

It was the ice beneath his feet. It moved.

"Uh . . . I think I need to get off this ice," he said to himself. "But which way is which? They all look the same!"

Then he heard a voice that sounded very much like Galen's.

. . . left . . . move left . . . three paces. Then turn right . . . five short steps . . . turn twice, crouch, and leap . . . leap . . .

"Wait!" said Eric. "Galen, is that you?"

Do what I said . . . .

"But it's too complicated. Say it again?"

Left three paces, the voice repeated.

He stepped left. "Okay . . ." he whispered.

Then right. Five short steps.

"How short?" asked Eric.

Short! said the voice. *Turn twice . . .*

Eric did that, then halted. He found himself standing at the edge of a chasm deeper than any he had ever seen.

"This doesn't look safe. Should I go back?"

No. You should leap.

"Leap? That's crazy. It's a bottomless pit!"

Trust me. And do it soon. They're after you.

"After me? Who's after me?"

All at once, Eric heard the cry of Yugs closing in behind him. *"Ayeee!"*

So are you going to leap?

"I guess I am!" said Eric.

Closing his eyes and holding tightly onto Galen's staff, he leaped into the chasm.

Faster and faster and faster he dropped, until the darkness around him was no more than a blur.

Six

In the Underground

Still clutching Galen's staff, Eric fell and fell and fell into the black chasm. The deeper and faster he fell, the more he felt as if he weren't actually *falling* so much as moving sideways or floating backward or drifting suspended in midair.

Time and time again, he tried to open his eyes, but wind was rushing too fiercely into his face. Finally, he forced one eyelid open.

"Are you kidding me?" he cried aloud.

He was not falling at all. He was moving forward through the air, no longer in a dark chasm, but in daylight, high in the air, and he was sitting in an elaborate leather saddle on the back of . . . of . . . of a giant flying creature.

A giant *blue* flying creature.

"The serpent!" he shouted. "The blue serpent! It's real. Holy cow. It's real! And I'm riding it!"

The serpent's neck arched up and down slowly as its great webbed wings rose and lowered in a slow, regular rhythm. And what at first looked like hinges or braces on the serpent's body, Eric decided was armor.

Clenching his knees tightly to the serpent's body, Eric looked down. Cold wind rushed against his face as he spotted a tall, broad hill surrounded by several smaller hills. In the distance, a great blue sea stretched far out to the horizon. With a certainty he could not explain, he knew the place below was his own town.

"So . . . this is my world?" he gasped.

It was his world!

The Upper World!

"But . . . how is it possible? My world doesn't have serpents —"

The serpent only cooed in response as if it were singing. "Roooo-*ooooo*!"

Below him he made out the houses and streets of his neighborhood.

"Woo-hoo!" he hollered. With a gentle nudge of his heels, he made the serpent loop over his house. He thought he saw a tiny figure in his yard waving up at him! Then the serpent circled over Neal's and Julie's rooftops. He laughed at the top of his lungs.

"This is *amazing!*"

"Roooo-ooooo!" the serpent cooed, louder than before.

As he petted the serpent's massive neck, he saw that its skin was covered with innumerable rows of scales the size and shape of snowflakes. His heart trembled inside him.

Then the serpent went up and up and did not stop climbing. No matter how often Eric nudged its sides, the serpent rose through the clouds toward a tunnel of dark air he had not seen before.

"Wait!" Eric shouted. "Turn back —"

Before he knew it, a storm surrounded them. Soon they were twisting and turning out of control. Thunder boomed. Lightning crashed all around. The serpent howled and swooped to avoid the jagged spears of light.

When lightning blazed, Eric spied vast ice fields and wastelands of snow. Towering mountains loomed over great frozen lakes.

"Droon?" he gasped. "Are we in Droon now? But how . . . ? Oh! We entered the passage!"

All of a sudden, a bolt of lightning shot down at him. He pulled the reins to try to turn the serpent, but there was no time. The searing flash struck the creature's neck, causing a deep wound, red and raw. It was exactly the size and shape of the snowflake treasure.

The treasure that was now gone.

"No!" cried Eric as the serpent faltered.

Then, instead of feeling alive and yielding, the creature's hide stiffened. The saddle was changing beneath Eric. The serpent's wings grew hard, immovable. What was happening?

Eric couldn't control the creature.

"Serpent!" he called out. Instead of its musically soothing voice, a mighty growl filled his ears. And the serpent was falling.

"We have to land!" Eric gasped, tugging on the reins as he had before, but to no effect.

The serpent fell, fell, fell, and just before it struck the ground, Eric saw everything dissolve — the serpent, the storm, Droon, everything — as if he had woken from a dream.

"Huh?" he gasped.

He was somewhere else. In darkness.

He lay in darkness.

Where was he?

Eric didn't know. Flexing his legs and arms, he realized he was lying on cold, hard ground. Was it the bottom of the chasm? Was it a cave of some kind? He rose to his feet.

"Hello?" he whispered.

There was no echo. He decided he must be in a small space. An inside space.

Slowly, he put his hand up. His fingers touched the ceiling. It was flat and smooth.

So . . . he was in a room?

"Of all the crazy things —"

There is a door. . . .

"What?" said Eric. "Who said that? Is somebody there?"

Me, as usual.

"And just who are you?"

Do you always have to argue? All I'm saying is that . . . there is a door. . . . Bye.

"Wait! Hello?"

There was no response.

Eric took a step. A gust of air moved across his face like a dry, thin scarf.

"A door?" he murmured. "Too weird."

Then he remembered Galen's staff. He felt around on the floor until he found it. Grasping it tightly in both hands, he uttered

a few words the wizard had taught him, and — *fwoosh!* — the staff lit up.

So he *was* in a room, and the room *was* small, but he felt strangely drawn to the wall on his left. Like the others, it was gray and solid and frosted with ice.

And yet . . . there was something about it.

No sooner had he set a hand upon it than he saw lines swimming across the wall in filigree patterns, twisting, turning, and looping back on themselves.

As Eric watched, all the lines came together into the outline of a low, round-topped door.

He trembled when he recalled the wizard's words — "Oh! Light!" — and his strange last look at him.

Then, all of a sudden, Eric's fingers sank into the rock and he fell headlong through the solid wall.

Seven

The Enchanted Room

Eric fell past the thick icy wall and into a space as blue as the evening sky.

He staggered but stayed on his feet, and was stunned at what he saw.

It was another room, but a room as enormous in size as it was impossible. The walls were several stories high and tapered to a rounded peak, as if he were standing inside a giant dome. Eric knew that the

walls were hewn from ice, yet they were pearly smooth to the touch.

Overhead, innumerable jewels, crystals, lights — *things* — twinkled across the ceiling's broad blue surface like stars.

When Eric took a step, the room hummed, as if the air itself were musical and his movement set it humming.

"Where am I —"

Swit! Swit! Swit! A bird — no, two birds — no, three birds! — glistening with crystalline wings swooped and banked around the ceiling, then settled into the limbs of a great tree he had not noticed before but that rose from floor to ceiling in the room's distant center.

As Eric approached the tree, it seemed to come nearer to him with each step, so that even though at first it seemed far away, in a very few steps, he was standing by its trunk.

"Okay, this is weird," he said.

The tree was leafless and sculpted, Eric imagined, of ice. But it was so intricate and detailed that its limbs, branches, and even twigs quivered from the movement of the bird's flight as if the tree were as impossibly alive as the birds.

"The enchanted room!" he whispered, afraid to raise his voice over the sound of the room's music. "I'm in the enchanted room the snowfolk told us about. But how could I be here? I fell through the ice miles from Krone. Did I fall so far? Have I actually found it? But . . . how is it possible . . . ?"

"A question I ask myself, too!" said a voice.

Eric whirled on his heels to see a blue-cloaked figure sitting cross-legged on the ground behind him. When the figure raised his head, Eric saw that it was Galen himself!

"Galen!" he exclaimed. He was sure he had passed the very same spot but had seen no one there. "But . . . how . . . I just . . ."

"I know," said the wizard. "I think you'll find that we keep moving around, much faster than is possible — oh, here we go!"

And suddenly, both he and Galen were sitting on a stout branch of the tree. It reminded Eric of the apple trees in his yard at home — trees that his dream vision had shown him only minutes before.

He blinked. "Where exactly are we?"

"I wonder," said Galen. "I fell through that wall — you saw me — and I ended up here. If you started from even farther away and fell here, too, all I can say is that this room truly *is* enchanted."

Eric smiled. "All roads lead to the enchanted room?" he said.

"Something like that," said the wizard,

who was holding a scroll that seemed to be made — like everything else — of ice.

"What's that?" Eric asked.

"A strange tale," said Galen, "of a poor young man who suffered a terrible accident and cannot remember his past. I found it in this room. These few words are all he was able to recall of his life before his memories left him completely. Touch it."

Eric obeyed, and at once he became aware of an odd sensation. The scroll seemed as alive as if he were holding the hand of the one who wrote it.

"Is it the story of the serpent master?" asked Eric. "I had a dream that I was riding the serpent. There was a terrible storm, and the serpent was struck by lightning. It lost a scale."

"The scale you have in your pouch right now," said the wizard.

Eric's throat thickened. Galen had to know about the treasure. How it was switched. Gone. How he had lost it. Slowly he opened the pouch. He removed the plain blue disc and held it to Galen. He swallowed. "The treasure —"

"Is safe," said the wizard. "Well done."

"But —"

"Promise me you will keep it safe," said Galen.

What? thought Eric. Could Galen not see what lay in his hand? But when Eric held up the disc, the clock face, the numbered dial — it was a blue snowflake once again.

"Strange to have lost a *part* of itself," said the wizard. "Almost as if the serpent were not so much *alive* as . . ."

Galen trailed off, then opened the scroll and ran his fingers slowly over the words as he spoke. "The serpent master's words are

sad," he said. "Listen. 'A storm. Lightning. I could not control her.'"

"Her?" asked Eric.

"I take him to mean the serpent," said Galen. He went on, "'I fell through the sky, my head wounded in the crash, remembering nothing of my life. I wandered this world for ages, my past a darkness to me, until I sensed her again in the far north. I found her below the ice. I made a home for the little ones. In exchange, they looked for her . . . treasure. Until it is found and the sky opens again, we cannot return home.'"

When Galen spoke, the room sang as if his words were notes plucked on an instrument. The song faded as his last words died away.

Eric breathed in deeply. "I think the serpent master sent me the dream and showed us how to find this room."

"But why not the others?" said Galen.

"Maybe we're the only ones who can help him return home," said Eric.

Galen slid down to the floor and began to pace. "Yes. Yes. He entered Droon through the storm. The serpent was — and is — his only way back to his own world — your world, Eric. But without the treasure, they cannot return." He turned to Eric.

"I fear these words could be the words of . . . could be my . . ." He paused, then spoke again. "These could be my brother's words. Urik was in the Upper World the last we know. What if he lost his memory? What if the prophecy . . ." Galen went silent.

Eric's heart thundered. The prophecy?

Yet as he stood beneath the lower branches of the tree and he looked straight through them to the underside of the dome, he felt something else.

Eric saw the three birds perched together on a high branch and, behind them, the room's far ceiling twinkling with the light of innumerable stars.

Birds. Stars. Birds. Stars.

What came to him then was so simple and yet so extraordinary.

"Galen," he said. "We know someone else whose words they could be. A man who lost his memory long ago. A man who wandered Droon for ages. Galen, the man who wrote those words could be the Prince of Stars!"

The old wizard gasped.

The Prince of Stars was a mysterious figure they had met once before in the far north. He was a man of clouded past. He had no memory. And he was accompanied by three birds.

"Yes!" cried Galen. "The Prince of Stars! Not Urik at all! The Prince of Stars!"

All at once, the birds began to sing, and the stars flashed. The entire room dissolved into a sparkling, whirling wind around the two wizards, and they found themselves on the stormy surface again.

Sudden shouts and the clatter of sticks sounded over the roar of snowfall.

"Ha-ha!" said Galen, twirling his staff high. "The dark prophecy? Ha! Ko loses today. Prince of Stars, indeed. There is power left in him still! My boy, we must hurry. Time passes. The storm reaches its peak. We must go from this place! And look there, your sled awaits its passengers. We have things to do!"

The two wizards, one young, one old, smiled broadly together.

"Save our friends!" said Eric. "Save the prince. And his blue serpent!"

Eight

Snow Racing!

The two wizards hopped onto the sled and surveyed the canyon.

"I see the others," said Eric. "Our friends are still fighting the Yugs."

"And losing," said Galen. "Are we ready?"

"Ready," Eric affirmed.

Together they leaned forward and — *whoosh!* — roared across the open snow to the children and the snowfolk. A band of

Yugs spotted them in a moment and hurled spears of ice as quickly as they could break them off their shoulders. Eric leaned from side to side, weaving the sled wildly.

"Eric!" yelled Galen, "do you have a license for this thing?"

Eric's laugh echoed across the wastes. "I'm learning as I go! More icemen behind us!"

"I see them!" Galen said. He whirled his blazing staff around, showered the Yugs with sparks, and fended off each new squad of attackers. *Flink! Crash! Bash!*

"Ha! The Prince of Stars! Of course!" the wizard cried. "Not Urik at all. I haven't felt this young in ages!"

A sudden flare rose in the distant sky, and the two wizards realized from its flowery shape that it was from Keeah.

"She's in trouble," said Eric. "Trade places."

As Galen took the driver's position, Eric clamped one hand firmly on the sled's railing. They flew over the snowdrifts, zigzagging around squads of Yugs. Soon they saw the stranded princess surrounded by dozens of shrieking ice warriors.

"Keeah, get ready!" Eric yelled. He leaned far out, nearly touching the snow. As Galen raced by, Eric grabbed Keeah's hand.

"Whoa!" she cried, skiing along behind the sled until Eric managed to swing her onboard. "Thanks for the ride!" she said. "The others are at the canyon pass!"

Eric saw two groups of ice warriors closing in on the sled from different directions.

"Hold on!" he shouted. Then he leaned into Keeah, forcing the sled into a spin that shot a blinding arc of spray at both bands of Yugs, pushing them backward.

"And now for our friends. Thrusters —

on!" said Galen, pointing his blazing staff behind the sled. It shot forward with the speed of a rocket, flying right over the ice warriors straight to the band of friends.

"Hooray!" yelled Max. "We are saved!"

Together, the spider troll, Julie, and Neal, along with Baggle and a handful of snowfolk, crowded onto the sled.

With barely a breath, Eric drove the sled toward the canyon pass, while Keeah and Galen together blasted at the snow that blocked the pass — *ka-boom-boooom!*

The snow dissolved, and the crowded sled flew onto the open ground outside.

"To Krone!" shouted Neal as they raced back to the ice city. "Save the snowfolk!"

But what they saw when they came within view of Krone stopped them cold.

The ice fields around the city were not barren as before. There were hundreds, thousands, tens of thousands of ice

warriors marching in step toward the walls. Not only that, groups of Yugs were dragging great ice cannons on sledges across the wastes. The cannons were aimed at the city's front gate, its most vulnerable spot.

"How will we get in?" groaned Max. "The whole army of Nesh warriors is here!"

"I can fly in over them," said Julie. "But I can't take us all in."

"The *Dragonfly*!" said Keeah. "Maybe my mother and Friddle have finished the repairs. We can fly over the army and right into the city. Hurry, let's find them."

Driving their sled to where the *Dragonfly* landed, they found Queen Relna and Friddle patching the last pieces of the plane together.

"How fares our ride?" asked Max.

"We know we can take off," said Relna. "We know we can fly. We can even steer. We're just not certain we can land."

"That's one of the major parts of flying," said Neal.

"The first rule of flying, as a matter of fact," said Friddle.

A loud cry went up. *"Ayeee!"*

Taking a spyglass from the plane, Galen mounted a snowdrift and looked back toward the city. "The Yugs have arrived at the gates," he said. "They await only the right moment to attack."

In the following silence, Eric heard a sound. *Tap . . . slish . . .* He looked around. Only Galen acknowledged his glance.

What is that? Eric asked him silently.

We'll know soon, said the wizard.

"Let's take our chances," said Keeah. "Friddle, fly us in there!"

Friddle jumped. "That's the spirit!"

Faster than it takes to say it, everyone crowded into the plane. One, two, three, the *Dragonfly* rumbled across the flat ice

plains and lifted. It wove a steady path up, up, up, until its passengers could see directly down into Krone.

A shriek rose from the Yug troops when they saw the plane. They hacked at the walls, using their hands as hatchets.

"That is the creepiest thing," said Julie.

"No argument here," said Neal.

Banking around, the *Dragonfly* finally dropped inside the city walls. With a bounce, a bump, a scrape, and a thud, the ship came to rest in the center of the village.

"Yes!" said Friddle. "We made it!"

Djambo and Mudji rushed to the passengers and helped them out of the plane.

Together, the two Orkins had done good work. Every wall was manned with snowfolk, each armed with a quiver of snowballs.

Relna called out, "Any remaining

snowfolk, split up. Those whose names begin with A through K, come with me to the east wall!"

"L through Q, follow me to the northern gate!" said Princess Keeah.

"The rest prepare campfires to melt snow into hot water," said Max.

"We'll help with that," said Mudji. "Set up urns at both eastern and northern gates."

As quickly as they could, the villagers organized into working brigades. They prepared snowballs and torches and candles and loaded sleds with more supplies in an unceasing train around the inside of the walls.

"Below us lies the enchanted room," said Galen. "We must defend the serpent and its master with all our powers —"

"The cannon!" shouted the snowfolk on the walls. "It aims. Duck! Now!"

With a terrifying shriek, the Yugs announced the first volley. The ice cannon blasted a great chunk of frozen snow. The northern gate shuddered from the impact.

A second blast came soon after, then a third and a fourth. Then came the sound of chipping and cracking at the gate. Galen led the largest company of snowfolk there. Eric and Neal were by his side.

All of a sudden, there came a blast from a different direction. It ripped across the air, resounding from one side of the city to the other.

A ball of ice the size of a house struck one of the jagged peaks that held the gate. The peak quivered and wavered, then toppled to the ground with a deafening roar.

With incredible speed the bony ice warriors poured through the broken wall.

They were inside the city.

Nine

The Green Flame

Shards of ice exploded into the city, cracking and shattering against houses.

Ayeeee! The icemen poured into the breach like a giant wave.

But Djambo, Mudji, and Max had prepared for this atop an ice tower near the gate.

At the spider troll's command — "Now!" — a dozen snowfolk tipped over a giant urn of hot water. It splashed swiftly

down the street before freezing into wild waves. The icemen tripped, struck the ground, and shattered into pieces. It took them minutes to reassemble. By then, more water was in place.

"Yahoo!" cried Max. "Do it again!"

Neal and Julie flew to the crumbled gate at the head of a troop of stick-wielding snowfolk. While the two children tossed volleys of snowballs from above, the little snowmen swung wildly with sticks.

"Yucky Yugs!" yelled Baggle, twirling his club. "Get them good!"

When the snowballs struck the ice warriors, the snow froze hard and formed heavy, ungainly armor over their bony frames. Under layer upon layer of frozen snow, the Yugs toppled and crashed to the ground.

"And now the candles!" cried Baggle. "Drop the candles!"

As yet another wave of Yugs charged in, the snowfolk on the top of the wall took aim and dropped hundreds of small parachutes. Tied beneath each one was a stout candle blazing with yellow flame. The ice warriors dodged to escape the flames, slowing their advance even more.

Knowing he couldn't muster more than a weak stream of sparks, Eric ran to help where he could. Then he felt a warm hand on his shoulder.

"Eric, come with me," Galen said. "There is someone we need to find. Do you still have the treasure safe?"

Eric's heart skipped a beat. He slipped his hand under his fur coat and squeezed the pouch. He didn't dare look inside.

"Right here."

"Our duty to the Prince of Stars is clear," said Galen. "Soon the storm will split the

sky, and the passage will open. We must hurry."

Eric glanced around, saw everyone occupied, and gave the old wizard a nod.

They ran together to a small ice mound at the center of the city.

"Is this the entrance?" said Eric.

"I believe it just as you do," said Galen. He pressed his hands upon the ice, and the outline of a doorway appeared.

The wizard smiled. "And in we go!"

With Galen's staff to light their way, the two fell together into the mound. Inside was a passage that led to more passages. Down, down, and down they went, from one rough staircase to another, into the heart of the underground. By the time they left the last step of the last stairway, the air was hushed and heavy.

"I douse my staff," said Galen, twisting

his hands. "From here we see with our hearts."

Fwish! The two friends were plunged into darkness. The sound of battle faded.

The sound of everything faded.

Silence.

Or was it silence?

Closing his eyes, Eric thought he heard a tiny sound.

Tap . . .

It was gone.

"Galen . . ." he whispered.

"I heard it," said the old wizard. "And down below, another sound. Moaning in the tunnels. The serpent lives, but barely. Eric, we shall solve this mystery together."

Eric felt that the wizard's voice was different. He spoke not as a mentor, not as a great old wizard, a champion of Droon, or a fighter for freedom, but as a friend.

An equal.

They stepped into the darkness, following the faint sounds. From one tunnel to the next, they went on until the passage opened up into a giant hollow cavern.

And they saw it.

A great silver dome rising to the ceiling of the cavern, lighting the air with its glow.

"The enchanted room!" whispered Galen. "How we two came here earlier, I cannot say. But it is the same room we visited before."

It was the same. They knew it instinctively.

The domed room stood on an island of stone, separated from them by a broad and bottomless chasm.

Galen stepped to the edge of the chasm and looked one way, then another, until he smiled.

"What is it?" asked Eric.

"An old trick," said Galen. "Come here, stoop low, and look across the edge."

When Eric did, he saw the nearly invisible shape of a bridge arching over the chasm.

"A bridge of ice!" Eric gasped. "Clever."

"Clever, indeed," said the wizard. "The Prince of Stars has picked up a wizard trick or two in his wanderings. I have seldom seen an invisible bridge made so well before."

With a deep breath, Galen set his foot out over the open chasm. It came to rest upon the invisible surface.

"Is it going to hold you?" asked Eric.

"I certainly hope so," said Galen. "Now, be careful and follow my steps. The bridge zigzags like a serpent's tail."

Galen seemed to know where to put his feet, and Eric followed. Before long,

the two wizards were across the invisible bridge and standing on the stone island.

The moment they reached safety, the tunnels on the far side of the invisible bridge rang with the sound of cracking sticks and shattering ice.

Max, Keeah, Julie, and Neal, along with Baggle and a handful of fellow snowfolk, rushed out of the tunnel. A troop of shrieking ice warriors was right behind them.

"Friends, crouch to the ground!" Galen shouted. With his staff, he fired a sizzling shot, which forced the Yugs back into the passage.

"Now come to us," said Galen. He sprayed a handful of dust on the bridge, making it visible for a few moments. The friends hurried across the bridge to the enchanted room.

"Those creepies will be back," said Julie.

"But not all the way," said the wizard. Then he took his staff and plunged it into the ice bridge. The bridge shattered and fell into the depths of the chasm.

"We have little time," said Max.

The moaning grew in Eric's ears like a song of pain. He knew that Galen heard it, too.

"We have no time!" said Galen, turning to the dome. "Eric, do the honors!"

Closing his eyes, Eric pressed his hands against the wall of the dome. Soon, his fingers found grooves his eyes could not see.

The Yugs shrieked again from the passage.

"Friends, be ready," said Keeah, her fingers flashing with violet sparks.

But when the Yugs entered the cavern, a flash of green flame sizzled in the air, too. The moment the ice warriors parted, a

dark figure stepped forward. He had twin horns blazing with green fire. He had four massive arms. He had the head of a bull, three dark eyes, and an armored body.

"Ko!" hissed Galen.

"I came to see the joyous prophecy fulfilled!" Ko boomed with a laugh.

"You fiend, you came for nothing!" said Keeah. She blasted the ground at Ko's feet.

"Eric — now!" said Galen.

Turning from Ko, Eric pressed hard on the icy wall and — *whoosh!* — he and Galen fell through to the other side.

Ten

A Wizard's Duty

As before, when Eric and Galen had entered the dome, it was impossibly larger than it seemed from outside.

As before, the ceiling gleamed with stars, the tree in the center of the chamber was exquisitely sculpted, and the birds — three of them — sat in its branches.

Only now, coiled beneath the silver tree was the enormous blue serpent.

Its giant head lay on the ground. Its neck, dotted with cutlass-sized spikes, seemed as lifeless as a stone. Its body, coiled around the trunk, was still, though every few moments it moaned in a soft, low tone.

Eric's heart thundered in his chest. "It's the same serpent I saw in my dream. The very same."

On the serpent's neck was a wound, raw and red and the very shape of the snowflake treasure he hoped was still in his pouch.

In the silence, Eric heard the voice, a bare whisper as if from a great distance.

Help us . . .

The old wizard shot him a look, and Eric knew that he had heard it, too.

All at once, the tip of the dome slid away, revealing the snow-lashed sky. Lightning flashed. Thunder rumbled without ceasing.

The storm was nearly at its peak.

"The treasure, quickly," said Galen.

His fingers quivering, Eric loosened the pouch string. He put his hand in and drew it out. The blue scale sat gleaming in his palm. *Thank you!* he thought. Breathing slowly to calm himself, he held out the snowflake to Galen.

"No," said the wizard. "It is yours to give."

"Mine? Why?"

"Go," said Galen. "Hurry."

Tentatively, Eric stepped to the serpent. It didn't move. He held on to a branch of the tree and climbed onto the creature's back. Its skin was cold. Only now, with his hands touching the beast, could Eric feel its labored breathing, slow, then quick, as deep as the earth, as shallow as a gasp. Carefully, he reached his hand out to insert the snowflake into the open wound on its back.

But the moment it touched the serpent's skin, the treasure was no longer a snowflake but the plain disc, the clockface dial with a blue button he had seen before.

"What? No . . . no . . ."

Dizziness overcame Eric. He felt cold and hot at the same time. Whether the creature's skin grew around the disk, whether it drew in a sudden breath of air, or whether he blacked out, he wasn't sure, but he slipped off and tumbled to the ground at Galen's feet.

Someone cried out from beyond the room.

Galen turned. "Our friends . . ."

Was it a cheer of victory? Was it a cry of distress? Eric could not tell. Galen went to the door. He passed through it amid more yells, leaving Eric alone.

"Wait. Don't go —"

Then he heard the voice again.

Thank you.

"Thank you . . ."

And a man was in the chamber with him.

If he *was* a man. He was more like a ghost. A fog. A mist in the shape of a cloaked man.

When he moved, sparks scattered from him like tiny stars, and the room filled with the sound of harp strings brushed by moving air.

When the man raised his head, his eyes, as green as emeralds, looked out from his cloak.

"The Prince of Stars," gasped Eric. "So it *is* you!"

"And what was lost is now restored," said the prince. "My serpent is cured."

His voice, thought Eric, was the very one he had heard leading him to the room

with the scroll. The prince approached the serpent, who now glowed with blue light.

With a wave of the prince's hand, the serpent uncoiled itself. Its massive wings lifted and stretched with a span so broad that they nearly touched the sides of the great room.

"Roooo-ooooo!" it cooed.

Eric gaped at the man, his mind reeling. "The last time we met, you had no memory of who you were. Do you even remember me? Do you still remember nothing?"

"I am a man," the cloaked figure said with a shake of his head. "A prince, they say."

"A prince with magic," said Eric, "who made all this, who can speak without making a sound, who flew a serpent from the Upper World — my world — all the way to Droon!"

The prince breathed slowly. "A wizard, then, cursed to remember nothing. For years,

I wandered Droon until I found my serpent here. I knew it was mine. Alas, it could not fly until what it had lost was found."

A thousand questions flooded Eric, and he wanted to blurt them all out at once. How exactly had the prince come here? Where had he been since they last saw him? How could he fly a serpent from his world to Droon a century ago when there *were* no serpents in his world?

But Eric could not utter a word.

For the sky cracked and crashed so violently above him that the whole dome shook. The next moment, Galen was there, his staff blazing. Keeah, Neal, Julie, Max, the Orkins, and the snowfolk were with him.

"Prince of Stars!" Galen said. "We cannot stop Ko's advance. We have little time. The passage between the worlds will open soon. You must return to your home —"

And then they heard it.

Tap . . . slish . . . tap . . . slish . . .

The sound came nearer with each passing moment until it was in the room with them.

Tap . . . slish . . .

A tall figure draped in filthy rags appeared at the far end of the chamber. He stabbed the earth with a sword, then pulled himself forward, detached the sword, stabbed it, and pulled himself forward again.

When he raised his cloaked head, they saw a gray face, a pointed gray beard. The man's eyes were dark, hollow, his ears . . . finless.

"Lord Sparr!" said Eric.

"Brother!" said Galen, rushing to the figure's side. Sparr now seemed far older than his older brother. "Why . . . why are you here?"

"I came as if driven by a force. I came . . . to atone for my sin," Sparr said. His voice was no more than a hoarse whisper.

"What sin?" asked Keeah.

"Long ago . . . I fought a noble brother. I stole from him. I escaped like a dog in the night. He followed me into a storm . . . the snow, the wind!"

The children knew what he meant. A long time before, Sparr had fought his brother Urik for the Moon Medallion and had stolen it.

"I do not see him," Sparr said, his head moving this way and that, blindly searching the room. "And yet I feel him. Is he here? Is it Urik, my brother?"

"No, no," said Galen. "It is not Urik. Because of the prophecy, I, too, feared it was so. But it is not he. It is the Prince of Stars. Your enemy once, but no longer."

"The prophecy . . ." said Sparr.

"Is unfulfilled," said Galen. "Unfulfilled! Our mother's sons are not all here —"

Ko's yells resounded outside the dome as blast upon blast struck the chamber door.

"Ko coming! Will not stop!" cried Baggle.

"I must go now," said the Prince of Stars. "Thank you all. Thank you, snowfolk, for caring for us all these years."

The prince climbed onto the serpent's back, touched the treasure, and grinned at Eric. "Thank you, Eric, for this. I may not know who I am, but I know I love to fly."

Eric saw a flicker of remembrance in the smile on the man's worn face. His emerald eyes, sad and dark, lit for a moment.

He whistled, and the three birds alighted on the saddle. "Serpent, imagine yourself a bird and fly, fly us back home!"

With a tug on the reins, the serpent lifted into the air.

Eric stared at the prince.

Terror struck him.

Thunder crashed, and the sky tore in two.

"The passage!" cried Keeah.

Ka—boooom! The dome's door shattered into nothing. Ko burst into the room at the head of a great band of ice warriors.

"Fly, Prince!" shouted Eric. "Fly now!"

"The prophecy!" boomed Ko. "The sons of Zara! Strike down the wizards! One shall fall!"

"But the prophecy is untrue!" yelled Galen. "Your prophecy has failed —"

It made no difference. At Ko's cry, three daggerlike icicles shot across the room.

Keeah and Galen together blasted the one aimed at the Prince of Stars. Relna

destroyed the icicle winging its way at Sparr. The third dagger shot across the room at Galen.

Eric tried to blast it, but nothing came from his fingers. "No!" he yelled.

He ran to Galen as fast as he could. He leaped to push the wizard clear, and the flying icicle pierced him in the shoulder.

Eric cried out and fell heavily to the ground. Pain surged through him like ice and fire.

"Eric!" cried Keeah. Wheeling on her heels, she blasted the Yug who had thrown the ice dagger, shattering him into pieces that would not combine again.

Ko's face showed shock. "The boy?"

Sparr, too, spoke. "The boy?"

Full of rage, Galen thrust his sparking staff at Ko again and again, hurtling the beast back beyond the chamber to the edge of the chasm. With one enormous blast, Galen

sent Ko into the dark hole. The emperor of beasts, howling at the top of his lungs, fell and fell and fell until he could be seen no more.

Eric lay on the ground, dazed, growing colder by the instant. Even as the dome's ceiling began to close above him, he glimpsed the blue serpent entering the crack in the sky.

What he saw then was that the serpent was not a serpent at all, but a thing of metal and cloth and wood, of wires and dials and bolts and rivets, of struts and wheels and wings, all curved and painted blue.

It was an airplane.

It was a very old plane from long ago, but not from the long ago of Droon.

It was an airplane from his own world.

At that moment Eric knew that a serpent never did fly to Droon from his world. He knew that the serpent master,

the Prince of Stars, the . . . man he saw was . . . an aviator.

An aviator whose plane reminded him of one he had seen in an old photograph of his mother's.

"No . . . no . . ." he breathed. "It can't be . . . it can't be . . ."

Eric saw the faces of his friends — Keeah, Galen, Neal, Julie, Max — hovering over him, their mouths moving but making no sound.

Then, whether their faces went away from him or he from them, he didn't know, for there was nothing.

For seconds, there was no sound. Then the rainbow staircase — the staircase from the Upper World to Droon — rippled into the dome, and Galen shouted, "Friddle! The *Dragonfly*! Neal and Julie, you must take the staircase home —"

"No way!" said Neal. "I'm not going anywhere. I'm not leaving my best friend!"

"You must go!" said Max. "The icemen will find the stairs. You must close it from above."

Julie shook her head over and over. "No . . . no . . . no . . ."

Together, the Orkins hustled Julie and Neal toward the staircase. The two friends didn't take their eyes off Eric for an instant.

"He's not moving!" said Julie.

"Come, come," said Djambo. "They will do what they can. Galen is the greatest of wizards. But he must take Eric to Jaffa City —"

Neal and Julie started up the stairs, keeping their eyes fixed on their friend.

Keeah held Eric's hand all the way to the airship. Her face was ashen, her cheeks

wet. "Eric, say something. Speak to me, please —"

Galen touched his fingers to Eric's forehead and trembled. "He is cold, cold. Eric is not with us right now."

"Oh . . ." Max whimpered.

Lord Sparr hurried with them, too, his own dark eyes moist with tears.

Moments later, the two planes had vanished on their separate journeys into the snow, one carrying a long-lost son of the Upper World to his destiny, the other hurrying Eric Hinkle to an uncertain fate.

As Julie and Neal approached the door to Eric's basement, their hearts were heavy with fear about the time ahead.

THE SECRETS OF DROON

By Tony Abbott

Read them all!

Under the stairs, a magical world awaits you!

Over 6.7 Million copies sold!

◼ SCHOLASTIC

www.scholastic.com/droon

DROONBL2